TOOTH FAIRY

With her cheery personality and her can-do attitude, the Tooth Fairy starts off every day with a smile! In her spare time, she likes to alphabetize her recipe cards and wrestle with grasshoppers.

Real Name: Esmerelda Floss

Place of Residence: London, England

Catchphrase: Ain't that the tooth!

Likes: Fresh breath, following rules, miming

Dislikes: Cavities

Strengths: Can change size, can fly, has sleeping fairy dust

Weakness: Bad breath ruins her day

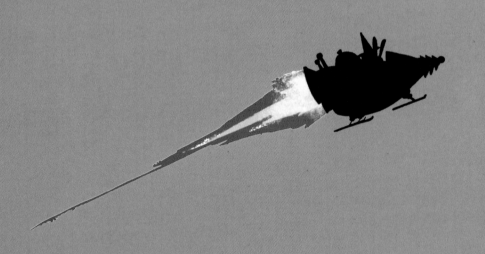

HOLIDAY HEROES SAVE CHRISTMAS

AUTHOR OF *HOW TO CATCH AN ELF*
ADAM WALLACE

PICTURES BY
SHANE CLESTER

sourcebooks
jabberwocky

Ho-ho-hold on, everyone. You are called *heroes* for a reason! You bring joy and laughter to children, and you each have unique talents! I need you to deliver presents on Christmas Eve!

US?!

Yes! Meet me at the North Pole at 0600 to begin your Christmas crash course training.

The fate of Christmas rests in your hands! Ho-ho-over and out.

The Heroes arrived at the North Pole, ready for their training. They learned as much as they could about being Santa:

It wasn't easy, but by the time Christmas Eve came, the Heroes were ready to save Christmas.

With a cheer and high-fives, the Heroes were on their way.

And so the Heroes went straight to work—but not everything went according to Santa's plan...

At the first house, the Easter Bunny hid the presents like it was an Easter egg hunt.

At the second house, the witch made the cookies disappear... by turning them into spiders!

At the third house, the Tooth Fairy hid gifts underneath all the pillows.

At the fourth house, the Leprechaun went to look for loose change.

Get back to the first house and sort this out!

Meanwhile...

The Holiday Heroes froze. Had they been spotted? Did they break their only rule? The Heroes knew they needed to fix this, and fast.

The Tooth Fairy used her sleeping fairy dust.

The Leprechaun used his super strength.

The Easter Bunny used his super speed.

And the Witch used a magic spell.

Once the Heroes reassembled, they looked at their hard work.
We did it!
Now only a bazillion other houses left.

By being themselves.

The Heroes improved at every house, and once the final present was placed under the final tree, it was time to head back to the North Pole.

WITCH

Having finally mastered her skills, the Witch no longer accidentally turns people into frogs—most of the time. She has won over 5,000 broom-flying races and always wins at guessing how many jellybeans are in a jar.

Real Name: Guinevere Spells

Place of Residence: Salem, Massachusetts

Catchphrase: Let's hocus this pocus!

Likes: Tarantulas, brewing potions, Christmas caroling

Dislikes: Snowmen

Strengths: Casting spells, mind reading, transforming into a lamp

Weakness: The sound of vacuum cleaners. Use a broom!

EASTER BUNNY

The Easter Bunny is a fierce little mammal with a huge case of optimism. He is arguably the best hip-hop dancer in the galaxy and holds the record for the most bubbles blown in 30 seconds (10,996 bubbles).

Real name: Eugene Rabbiton
Place of Residence: Easter Island
Catchphrase: Let's hop to it!
Likes: Smiling, eating hardboiled eggs, extreme pogo stick jumping
Dislikes: Gray clouds
Strengths: Super speed, supersonic hearing, can hold his breath for 58 minutes
Weakness: Bad attitudes of any kind